DETECTIVE
NOSEGOODE
and the
MUSEUM ROBBERY

DETECTIVE
NOSEGOODE

and the
MUSEUM ROBBERY

Marian Orłoń

Illustrated by Jerzy Flisak

Translated by Eliza Marciniak

PUSHKIN CHILDREN'S BOOKS

Pushkin Press
71–75 Shelton Street
London, WC2H 9JQ

Original text © Maria Orłoń 2013
Illustrations © Piotr Flisak and Mikołaj Flisak 2013
English translation © Eliza Marciniak 2017

Detective Nosegoode and the Museum Robbery was first published as
Jak detektyw Nosek zadziwił Lipki Nowe, 1976

Published by arrangement of Wydawnictwo Dwie Siostry, Warsaw (Poland)

First published by Pushkin Press in 2017

10 9 8 7 6 5 4 3 2 1

ISBN: 978 1 782691 59 4

Designed and typeset by Tetragon, London
Printed and bound by TJ International Ltd. Padstow PL28 8RW

www.pushkinpress.com

THE MUSEUM ROBBERY

Detective Ambrosius Nosegoode – a famous resident of Ashworth feared by criminals everywhere – was tugging at the few hairs left on his head and mumbling something under his breath. On the desk in front of him lay a newspaper with a half-solved crossword puzzle. It was this crossword that was the cause of all the hair tugging and unintelligible muttering. In one corner of the room Cody the dog was lying on a patterned rug and watching his master with amusement.

Mr Nosegoode caught Cody's amused look and burst out, "If you're so smart, tell me what this is: 'More valuable than gold; more faithful than one's own shadow'."

Cody slowly yawned and replied casually, "It couldn't be more obvious: a dog."*

"A dog, did you say?" the detective livened up. He bent over the crossword, counted the squares and exclaimed, "It fits! Congratulations! You're amazing!"

* Readers familiar with the previous two books about Mr Nosegoode – *Detective Nosegoode and the Music Box Mystery* and *Detective Nosegoode and the Kidnappers* – will already know that Cody has perfect command of the human language. It should be noted that the three adventures described in this book take place earlier than those in the previous two books – before Mr Nosegoode retired and moved with Cody to Lower Limewood.

Cody nodded with an indulgent smile.

"A person who takes so long to realize that his dog is amazing does not deserve to have such a dog."

"Are you giving me a hard time?" Mr Nosegoode asked in an offended voice.

"No. I'm being philosophical," the dog replied and stretched out on the rug.

Mr Nosegoode shrugged and bent over the crossword again.

"Empty-headed and..." he muttered.

The dog leapt up onto all fours.

"I beg your pardon? I object!" he growled.

Mr Nosegoode blinked in surprise.

"What do you object to?"

"This talk about my head. What's in it is my own business."

Mr Nosegoode burst out laughing.

"Cody, my friend!" he chuckled. "I have an excellent opinion of your head, believe me!"

"So why are you talking rubbish, about how it's empty?"

"I'm not talking rubbish. That's the next cross-word clue."

"What a silly donkey I am!" Cody said as he also snorted with laughter.

They laughed together, as they often did in their small, cheerful flat in Lilac Street. This time, however, their merriment was cut short by the shrill ring of the telephone. They fell silent and exchanged puzzled looks.

"Who could it be?" Ambrosius wondered out loud, walking over to the phone.

The dog followed.

"Hello?" the detective answered.

"Is this Mr Ambrosius Nosegoode?" an unfamiliar voice in the receiver asked.

"Yes, that's me," Ambrosius confirmed.

"Inspector!" The breathless voice shouted so clearly that Cody could hear every word. "We need your help! If you don't help us, something terrible might happen..."

"I'm sorry," Ambrosius interrupted a bit impatiently, "but I don't know with whom I have the pleasure..."

"Oh, I'm the one who should apologize!" said the unidentified speaker, who was suddenly embarrassed. "I've completely lost my head. My name is Vincent Fiddlestick. I'm the director of the Ashworth Museum."

"Good morning, Mr Fiddlestick," Ambrosius said, automatically bowing. "Now, please tell me calmly what danger is looming over your head."

"It's not over *my* head!" Vincent Fiddlestick quickly protested. "There's something far more valuable than my head that's in danger! What is at stake is an outstanding work of art, the pride of our museum – the famous painting of Ashworth at sunset by Bonaventure Splotch!"

Ambrosius gave Cody a meaningful look, to show that this was a serious matter indeed, and continued listening attentively to the director's story.

"About an hour ago," the voice from the receiver went on, "two unidentified individuals appeared at the museum. They showed suspicious interest in this specific painting, and I'm sure that..."

"Just a second," interrupted the detective, not letting him finish, "couldn't they just have been ordinary art lovers? Bonaventure Splotch's masterpiece is so beautiful that it's hard to walk past it without paying it any attention."

"That's out of the question!" the director said decisively. "I can tell an art lover from a mile off. A true art lover, Mr Nosegoode, is sure to notice other precious works of art, of which we have plenty in our museum. But not those two. They walked past them as if all the other works on display were cabbages at a market stall! They didn't stop until they got to *Ashworth at Sunset*, and then they whispered in front of it for a while. And there's more. Our doorman, who happened to be walking by, heard something which leaves no doubt about their intentions."

"What was it?" Mr Nosegoode interrupted the director again.

"'We have to nab it tonight'," the director said.

This made a strong impression on the detective.

"I see," he said. "It sounds like your fears are well founded. I will deal with these villains. Just tell me what they look like and where I can find them."

"What they look like? Hmm..." the director was flummoxed. "They look completely normal; there's nothing unusual about them. But they differ in height: one is over six feet tall, while the other barely comes up to his shoulders. As for where to find them, my guess is that they're at the Hambone Inn. They were heading in that direction a few minutes ago."

"Thank you, that's all I need to know," Mr Nosegoode said. "I'll go there straight away and discreetly keep an eye on them. Take heart, Mr Fiddlestick! We won't let them steal our treasure!"

"Let's hope for the best!" Vincent Fiddlestick declared emotionally.

Mr Nosegoode hung up the receiver and turned to his dog.

"Did you hear all that?" he asked.

"Yes, every word," Cody said.

"So, off to the Hambone Inn!" the detective commanded.

Cody licked his lips.

"Happily! There are few places on earth I love as much as that friendly pub."

And so they went.

The Hambone Inn occupied the ground floor of an old building in Singing Starlings Place. It was famous among local dogs and their owners because it was the only establishment in town that welcomed every Rover, Fido and Spot regardless of breed, shape or size. Dogs were not only allowed but were positively encouraged to come inside. "Dogs warmly welcome!" announced the big sign on the door, inspiring genuine fondness in every dog's heart.

This wasn't the only sign that adorned the outside of the pub. There was another, at the sight of which Cody's mouth watered instantly. It advertised the speciality of the house: bones simmered in butter – Cody's favourite dish. It was no wonder that deep down inside he was almost grateful to the suspicious admirers of Bonaventure Splotch.

They stepped inside and looked around the room. Portraits of distinguished-looking canines gazed down at them from the walls, and no less distinguished-looking men and women sat at the tables – under which the cream of the crop of dog society was busy chewing on bones.

As Cody scanned the room for acquaintances, Ambrosius looked for the admirers of the treasured painting. He had no problem identifying them: they were the only customers who were not accompanied by a dog, which was an obvious giveaway. They sat in the corner of the room, sipping beer and discussing something excitedly. The fact that there were no free tables anywhere near them made Ambrosius's task of spying on them rather difficult.

Luckily, I have a dog, he thought, taking a seat at a table beside a large tile stove. Reassured, he bent down and spoke directly in Cody's ear, while pretending to tie a shoelace.

"They're here. They're sitting in the corner, whispering feverishly. We must not let them out of our sight. Try to get close to them. So as not to arouse their suspicions, act as though you want to play with that friendly puppy hanging around their table. Go now – and good luck!"

Cody nodded to show he'd understood. Wagging his tail amiably, he strolled over to the young dog. They met next to the muddy shoes of one of the suspects and quickly started having fun together.

Ambrosius watched them for a moment, but he was interrupted when a waiter approached to take his order.

"Good day to you, Inspec..." He bowed and broke off abruptly when the detective gestured for him to stop.

"I understand," the waiter winked at Ambrosius knowingly. "It's good to see you again. What can I get you?"

"A small black coffee and a bone simmered in butter please," Mr Nosegoode said. "A big one!" he added with emphasis.

The waiter bowed again and hurried off to the kitchen.

Ambrosius pulled *The Voice of Ashworth* out of his pocket, unfolded it like a screen in front of him and resumed watching Cody.

If he didn't know better – if he wasn't aware of just how seriously Cody treated his every request – he would have thought that the dog had forgotten all about his instructions. He seemed to be having a great time, not paying the least attention to the two men whispering above him. But Ambrosius knew his dog, and he had no doubts as to what lay behind this carefree play.

He wasn't mistaken. Cody romped about and frolicked just as much as his new young friend, but at the same time he strained his ears to catch every word. The first thing he heard confirmed his suspicions: the two strangers were preparing a cunning plan to rob the museum! Vincent Fiddlestick had been right to worry about the fate of the most precious canvas in his collection, and he'd been right to ask Detective

Nosegoode for help: the robbers really did have their eyes on the treasured painting.

Their discussion lasted about a quarter of an hour. Then the two thieves clinked their glasses in a toast to the success of their plot, drank the last of their beer and left the pub.

When the door closed behind them, Cody said goodbye to his friendly companion, who was disappointed that the fun had come to an end, and sprinted back to Ambrosius.

"So?" the detective asked quietly, pretending to be completely absorbed in his newspaper.

"Sensational news!" Cody whispered back. "A real bombshell! I know their plans for the robbery! I'll tell you everything once we're outside. Now how about that bone?"

"It's on its way."

And indeed, just at that moment the waiter came up to the table, carrying a cup of coffee in one hand and a plate with a huge bone in the other.

"Doesn't it look delicious?" he said as he presented the dish. "You know," he turned to Mr Nosegoode, "sometimes I wish I were a dog."

Mr Nosegoode laughed cordially, while Cody looked at the waiter with interest. He soon turned his attention to the bone, however, since he knew people too well to take everything they said seriously.

He finished his meal surprisingly quickly, while

Ambrosius also drank his coffee in record time, and they were soon out on the street again.

"Tell me!" the detective could hardly wait.

Cody looked all around to make sure they were alone and then related the details of the devious plan to steal the painting. The detective listened, shaking with indignation. When the dog reached the end, he burst out, "What scoundrels! Thieves! Cunning foxes! We'll see who outwits whom! I'll teach them such a lesson that they'll remember our Splotch for the rest of their lives! Let's get started, my friend."

Cody looked at him with admiration.

"What are you planning to do?" he asked.

"You'll soon see. Let's go and talk to Director Fiddlestick. I have a great deal to tell him."

As they approached the museum, which was located in the centre of a large park, the clock on the nearby church tower struck four.

*

A while later, the early autumn evening enveloped the town like a dark cloak. In the main room of the museum, the lights were still on, but then the door-man appeared, jangling his keys, and began switching off the lamps one by one. He did this every day when the old grandfather clock showed six. As he walked past Bonaventure Splotch's painting, which hung in the place of honour, he paused for a moment, and something like a sly smile crossed his face.

After turning off all the lights, he shuffled down the corridor leading to the exit, sighed deeply and sat down on top of a richly decorated treasure chest not too far from the door.

"Oh, old age! One gets tired more and more easily," he muttered loudly and noiselessly turned the key that was sticking out of the lock on the front of the chest.

He complained a bit more about his various ailments and then, with the same sly smile with which he'd looked at Splotch's painting, he trundled off towards the exit. The door creaked, a key made a grating sound in the lock and silence fell in the museum.

But not for long. A few minutes later, something very peculiar started happening inside the antique chest. Rustling and tapping could be heard, and then the lid groaned, as if someone were trying to lift it from the inside. This sound came a few more times before somebody swore and said, "He locked me in! The old geezer's locked me in!"

*

Around the same time, a horse-drawn cart stopped in front of the museum, and three men and a dog jumped down to the ground while the driver remained in his seat. The three men were Detective Nosegoode, Vincent Fiddlestick and Constable Stork. The dog, of course, was Cody.

The three evening visitors were greeted by the old doorman, who came out from behind a tree and said, "All done."

"The fox is in the trap?" Mr Nosegoode enquired.

"I think so. I didn't check, but I heard some rustling as I was locking the chest."

"What about the other one?"

"I let him leave. Just as you asked, Inspector."

"Did he by any chance say where he was going?"

"No."

"That's fine. You've done a great job."

The doorman blushed at this compliment, and the detective addressed them all.

"Gentlemen! From this moment on, we need to forget who we are and start acting like master thieves."

"Like thieves?!" the museum director blurted out, shocked.

"Yes," Mr Nosegoode confirmed. "Like thieves."

Mr Fiddlestick had a funny look on his face.

"I'm sorry..." he mumbled, "but I'm afraid I don't understand..."

"Let me explain!" Ambrosius lowered his voice and continued. "The criminals we're dealing with are clever. Or at least one of them has earned the right to be thought of as such. If we accuse them of plotting to steal Bonaventure Splotch's painting without being able to prove it, they will deny it. When the one who's sitting inside the chest realizes who we are, he will no doubt make up some tale as an excuse. For example, he might say that someone had locked him in as a practical joke, or that it was a silly bet, or maybe he'll come up with some other story. What will we do then? That's why we need to use a trick to get the truth out of him. We have to find out where his partner in crime – the mastermind behind this whole plan – is waiting. So, in order to do that, we'll pretend to be thieves ourselves."

"What a brilliant idea!" Vincent Fiddlestick exclaimed in delight.

"Brilliant!" echoed the others.

They decided to do a little practice run of the performance that was about to take place at the museum. Ambrosius assigned roles and gave acting tips, while Cody sat off to the side and tried to imagine the forthcoming meeting with the thief, replaying in his mind the conversation he had overheard at the

Hambone. He could almost see the two faces bent over the table and hear the words they had spoken...

*

"I have an idea, Doughnut!" the taller of the two thieves, whom Ambrosius had just described as the mastermind behind the robbery, had said. "There's an old treasure chest in the corridor by the door. A large, antique chest. All you have to do is slip inside without being noticed and Splotch will be ours."

The thief nicknamed Doughnut evidently wasn't blessed with a rich imagination because he couldn't for the life of him understand what the chest had to do with Splotch.

"What do you mean by 'All you have to do is slip inside without being noticed and Splotch will be ours'? I don't get it," he confessed with disarming honesty.

The one in charge – who, as it later turned out, was nicknamed Beanpole – smiled indulgently and began to explain.

"My plan goes like this. Towards evening, I'll pop by the museum and start chatting with the doorman. We'll be by the front door at first, but then I'll get him to come with me to the main room. I'll start talking hogwash – about how I love painting, how I can't live without art and so on."

"You think he'll swallow it?" Doughnut asked doubtfully. "You don't look like someone who can't live without art."

Beanpole straightened up in his chair.

"I don't? Well, once I've shaved and splashed on some cologne and put on a tie, I could even pass for a professor!"

This was too much for Doughnut: he couldn't keep a straight face.

"Professor Beanpole!" he started choking with laughter. "Ha ha ha, you're killing me!"

"Shut up, Doughnut, and listen to me carefully, or I might lose my temper!"

Beanpole's sugar-sweet tone sounded so threatening that Doughnut instantly stopped laughing.

"All right, all right..." he muttered. "Go on."

"Wait... Where was I?"

"You were saying how you'll start talking hogwash," Doughnut reminded him.

"Right! So. I'll keep the old man busy with all sorts of hogwash, and in the meantime you'll slip into the corridor, walk over to the treasure chest, lift the lid and dive inside. You'll lie down, like in your own cosy bed, close the lid and wait until evening."

Doughnut stared at him blankly.

"Why do I have to wait until evening?"

"Why?! So that we can steal the painting!" Beanpole exploded.

"Can you... Can you explain it more clearly?"

"Fine. You will sit, or rather lie, inside this chest until the museum closes. Once the doorman has locked up and left, you will come out of the chest, grab Splotch off the wall, wrap the picture in some rags and come to meet me. I'll tell you where we're going to meet later."

"And just how exactly am I supposed to get out of the museum if the door is locked?" Doughnut dared to ask.

Beanpole looked at him with appreciation.

"A very sensible question, Doughnut. But I wouldn't be the cunning Beanpole if I didn't have an answer. The museum has an emergency exit that is bolted from the inside. All you need to do is slide the bolt and you'll be free to go."

"In that case, can't we slide the bolt during the day and then enter through that door at night?"

"No, we can't," Beanpole replied decisively. "The doorman is sure to check all the doors before he leaves. Anything else you're not sure about?"

Doughnut finally looked like he was thinking hard about something.

"But what if..." he began uncertainly. "What if someone finds me inside that chest? Anything could happen. What do I do then?"

"Nobody is going to find you!" Beanpole said with unshaken confidence. "Why would anyone look in there? But just in case, we can come up with an explanation. Leave it to me."

"Hmm. Why don't you climb into that antique coffin yourself," Doughnut suggested slyly, "and I'll wait for you outside."

Beanpole gave him a pitying look.

"Have you gone mad?" he said. "I'm six foot three! I'd have to fold in half like a penknife to fit inside."

"All right, no need for excuses," Doughnut sighed. "Clearly I'm the one who's going to crawl inside that stupid box."

"You won't regret it!" Beanpole breathed a sigh of relief. "We'll get a big pile of cash for that doodle. We're going to be rich, Doughnut!"

*

Cody snapped out of his thoughts when he saw Ambrosius gesture to him that the rehearsal was over and that they were about to go inside. He followed. They entered the museum cautiously and started creeping towards the antique chest. The detective, the director, the doorman and Constable Stork were all behaving like professional robbers, carrying torches and speaking in low voices. They made sure, however, that their words could be heard inside the treasure chest.

"It's over there in the corner. Do you see it?" Ambrosius said, pointing to the chest.

"Yes, I see it," Vincent Fiddlestick replied in a hoarse voice, since he believed that this was how any self-respecting robber ought to sound. "A nice piece of work!"

"Handmade in Poland," Constable Stork croaked in a similar tone.

"Quick, lads, let's grab it and be off!" Ambrosius hurried them along. "A good thief thinks long but acts fast. That's what the famous Felonius Crampbark, also known as Picklock, used to say."

They grasped the chest by the handles but let go almost instantly.

"It's so heavy!" Ambrosius grumbled. "Hey, maybe there's treasure inside?"

"Let's check!" Vincent Fiddlestick said eagerly.

"Right now? There's no time," Constable Stork scolded him. "Remember what Felonius Crampbark said? A good thief acts fast. We'll check later, back at our hideout."

As they got ready to lift the chest again, they finally heard what they had all been waiting for. Something banged around inside, and a faint, pleading voice came from within.

"Friends! It's me, Doughnut, your fellow thief! Open the chest! I've also got a little job to do here."

They exchanged knowing glances, and Ambrosius spoke first.

"Oh yeah, but what kind of a job is it, pal? You might be a fellow all right, but how do we know you're a thief! You could be a copper for all we know. Maybe this is your bizarre way of guarding this dump, huh?"

"No way!" Doughnut was offended. "I'm an honest thief, for the love of money! Open up!"

"Well, well, isn't he demanding," Ambrosius sneered. "Why don't you open it yourself?"

"I can't!" Doughnut groaned. "That's the whole problem."

"Why? Are you feeling faint or something?" Ambrosius sounded concerned.

"No, no, I'm not feeling faint. But I've been locked inside. With a key."

"Who locked you in?" the detective feigned surprise.

"The doorman. That horrid old codger."

The doorman turned bright red, and if Ambrosius hadn't stopped him, he would have started pounding on the treasure chest with his fists.

"So he knew you were inside?" the detective continued his questioning.

"No. How could he? Come on, open up!"

"Just a minute. I need to have a look at the lock."

Ambrosius leant down and started fiddling with the locking mechanism.

"No can do," he said after a pause. "The lock is antique and too strong. We'd have to break it, but we don't have the tools. We'll open it once we get to our hideout."

"But I have work to do here!" Doughnut wailed tearfully.

"Don't worry. The work will still be there tomorrow," Mr Nosegoode remarked philosophically.

"Don't joke!" Doughnut pleaded. "I have to get some wretched painting out of here, or my friend Beanpole is going to go ballistic."

"Ah, that's a different story. You should have told us about the painting from the start!" Ambrosius changed his tone. "We can help you. We'll take down the painting ourselves and deliver it to your pal, with you in tow. So, which painting is it, and where's your mate?"

"I don't know how to thank you!" Doughnut was deeply touched.

"Thank us?" Ambrosius said in a magnanimous tone. "What for? We have to help each other in misfortune, don't we? Professional solidarity, my friend! So, which painting is it?"

"The biggest one, on the left. Painted by Stain or Splotch or something."

"All right, we'll find it. And your mate?"

"He's waiting at The Pickled Herring. Next to the train station."

"Well, it doesn't matter now," Ambrosius declared. "Hey, Vince!" he called to the director. "Go and nab that picture off the wall, and we'll get ready to haul this box away!"

The director's eyes nearly popped out of his head, but he quickly got into his role and replied in a servile tone, "Right on it, boss!"

He winked at Mr Nosegoode, ran off to the main room, gazed tenderly at his beloved canvas for a few moments, then came running back and reported, "All done!"

"Excellent. Let's grab the box and get outta here!" commanded Ambrosius, who was becoming more and more amused.

Grunting, they heaved the chest up, lugged it outside and put it in the horse-drawn cart. Before setting off, Ambrosius called Constable Stork to one side and whispered something in his ear. The policeman nodded and walked off in the direction of the train station. Ambrosius climbed on top of the treasure chest, behind the driver, where Vincent Fiddlestick and the doorman were already sitting, and settled in next to Cody.

"To our hideout!" the detective called out just in case, although the driver knew perfectly well where he was supposed to go.

The whole band of robbers turned out to be rather untalkative during the ride. About a quarter of an hour later the cart stopped in front of a brightly lit building. There was a blue sign on the outside that read:

POLICE STATION
— ASHWORTH —

Ambrosius tapped on the lid of the chest.

"We're here," he announced.

"Finally!" Doughnut was relieved.

It didn't take them long to carry the chest inside. They placed the heavy antique in the middle of the room, where a kindly sergeant was already waiting for them, and began preparing for the big event: the release of Doughnut. The honour fell to Mr Nosegoode. It was a solemn moment.

In the total silence that filled the room, Ambrosius strode over to the chest, turned the key in the lock and with one determined movement opened the lid. From within, Doughnut sprang up like a jack-in-the-box, sweating profusely. He had clearly forgotten about the antique lock that had to be broken using tools.

"Freedom at last!" he cried out and looked happily at those gathered around him.

All of a sudden, he noticed the sergeant's uniform and nearly fainted. His face turned white, his eyes widened in astonishment and his lips started moving soundlessly. The sergeant's words were the final straw.

"Welcome, Doughnut!" the kindly guardian of the public order called out to him in an almost fatherly tone. "How was your journey?"

He didn't receive a reply. Doughnut couldn't utter a word.

"Come now, why are you so surprised?" the sergeant laughed heartily. "You don't like the company? Don't worry! We'll find you more suitable companions."

As if to confirm his words, the door swung open and Constable Stork appeared, gently pushing none other than Beanpole into the room. Beanpole, not realizing what had taken place over the course of the previous hour, had a confident expression on his face and was acting like the embodiment of innocence, persecuted by brutal policemen. Only when he saw Doughnut did he understand what had happened and appeared to wilt on the spot.

"Well, Beanpole, aren't you glad to see Doughnut?" the sergeant pretended to be surprised.

But Beanpole wasn't in the mood for jokes. He'd been caught – and he knew what that meant.

The sergeant was also done with jokes. He stopped smiling. His face hardened and his voice sounded forbidding as he said to Constable Stork, pointing to Doughnut and Beanpole, "Enough of these games! Lock them up! And bring them for questioning first thing in the morning."

"Yes, sir!" the constable straightened up. He grabbed the two would-be robbers by their shoulders and led them out of the room.

"That's enough for today," the sergeant said, taking a deep breath and wiping his forehead with a large chequered handkerchief. He thought about something for a moment and turned to Mr Nosegoode.

"There's one thing I'd like to ask you about, Inspector," he said. "How did you discover their clever plan? Surely they didn't confide in you, did they?"

Ambrosius smiled mysteriously.

"Of course not," he replied. "But I have my methods..."

As he said these words, he looked fondly at Cody, who assumed the humblest of expressions and casually watched a fly circle around the ceiling lamp.

A GAME OF CHESS

Ambrosius Nosegoode loved summer evenings. He would throw the windows wide open, breathe in the scents from neighbouring gardens, listen to the singing of the birds and – perhaps inspired by it – pick up his flute and devote himself to music. Cody would sit at his feet and gaze at the distant moon, longing for something he couldn't put into words.

This evening was no different. A wistful melody poured forth from the flute, and Cody was lost in faraway thoughts, when all of a sudden there was a knock on the front door. Ambrosius wasn't expecting any visitors, and in any case it was too late for social calls, so he looked somewhat surprised as he got up and went out into the hallway. He unlocked the door – and found himself face to face with a stranger. The man was short, with a long, sharp nose and sly eyes. He glanced left and right and, without waiting for an invitation, slipped inside.

"Are you alone?" he asked in a secretive whisper.

Mr Nosegoode looked him up and down and answered coolly, "Don't you think that I should be the one to ask the first question?"

"I'm sorry," said the newcomer, remembering his manners, "but there's a very delicate matter I'd like to discuss with you, and I'd prefer not to have any witnesses. May I come in?"

"Please."

The visitor eagerly followed Ambrosius into the main room, cast a snooping glance all around and noticed Cody.

"Is that your dog?"

"Yes. He's my friend," Mr Nosegoode emphasized the last word, and Cody nodded, as if to confirm this claim.

"And there's nobody else here?"

The detective had difficulty controlling his impatience.

"Nobody. Unless you want to count three spiders and a mouse."

The visitor looked a bit hurt by this response.

"You're joking, but I've come to you with a serious problem," he said.

"I'd be glad to find out what that is," Mr Nosegoode replied.

"You will in a minute, but first let me introduce myself."

"It would be my pleasure," Mr Nosegoode bowed.

"My name is Telesphorus Greylag. I have a passion for board and parlour games," the visitor began in an unusually lofty tone.

Mr Nosegoode bowed again.

"I can say without any false modesty," the game enthusiast continued, "that I've even achieved some distinction in that field. For the past year, I've held the prestigious position of treasurer at the Ashworth Chess Club, and just last month I received the Golden Pawn Award at the chess tournament in Little Hoofton. And that's not all. It looked very likely that I would be chosen to be president of our club in the upcoming elections. A glorious career lay ahead of me – until now. A dark shadow has suddenly been cast over my spotless reputation, and my future hangs in the balance."

"But why?" Ambrosius exclaimed.

"Because," Telesphorus Greylag lowered his voice, "somebody broke into the cash box at the club and stole an entire year's worth of membership fees!"

"Yes, that's a very unpleasant matter indeed," the detective admitted. "But I don't understand your worry. Why would your reputation suffer on account of some burglar if you haven't done anything wrong? Unless you've neglected your duties in some way?"

The visitor shook his head.

"No, not at all, I haven't neglected anything. But you know how people are. Some of them just can't wait for another person's bad luck. It won't be long before there are rumours, suspicions, mistrust... That could be the end of my career!"

Ambrosius took out his pipe and began filling it carefully. Telesphorus Greylag watched him with visible anxiety.

"So you've come to me..." Ambrosius said at last.

"Yes. I've come to you," the visitor continued, "so that you can help me prove that I have nothing to do with this whole business and that I can't be blamed for it!"

Ambrosius lit his pipe and puffed on it a few times, filling the room with aromatic smoke. Then he said, "And here I was thinking that you had come to ask for help with catching the thief..."

"That too, of course!" Greylag quickly assured him. "Only I'm afraid that..."

"What are you afraid of?" the detective looked at him keenly.

Greylag seemed uneasy.

"I'm sorry, but I fear that it will be easier to save my reputation than to find the thief."

Ambrosius lifted his pipe to his mouth again and smiled mysteriously.

"I see that you underestimate Detective Ambrosius Nosegoode," he remarked modestly.

"I don't! I wouldn't have come here if I did. But how could you find one criminal among the thousands of residents of Ashworth if that person has left no traces?"

"Are you sure there are no traces?"

Greylag nodded.

"I went there today," he said. "I searched the room thoroughly and found nothing at all. There's only the empty cash box with its broken lock."

A little cloud of aromatic smoke formed over the detective's head.

"Perhaps I will have more luck," he said.

"You want to go there yourself?"

"Of course. My great teacher and friend Hippolytus

Whiskers used to say that only ghosts leave no traces – people always do. If I'm to help you, I have to go and see your club room."

Telesphorus Greylag hesitated for a split second before admitting, "Indeed, I might have missed something. I'd be grateful if you could pop by. When can you come?"

Ambrosius glanced at his watch.

"Right now," he answered unexpectedly.

"Right now?" the visitor said, surprised. "But it's late at night, and I wouldn't want to trouble you..."

"Oh, it's nothing," Ambrosius cut him off. "For a detective, it's never too late; there's no such thing as bad weather or tiredness... Duty always comes first."

He excused himself and went with Cody to the neighbouring room to get ready. When they were alone, he asked the dog, "So? Do you have any suspicions?"

"Hmm... I have the beginnings of an idea..." Cody answered cautiously.

"Me too," Ambrosius said.

They smiled at each other knowingly.

Half an hour later, the three of them – Mr Nosegoode, Cody and Telesphorus Greylag – stopped in front of a door marked with a brass plate that read:

ASHWORTH CHESS CLUB

Before they went inside, Ambrosius examined the door thoroughly, paying special attention to the lock. He shone his torch on it and inspected it closely with his magnifying glass.

"Hmm! Not a scratch," he muttered when he was finished. "This means that the burglar either had a spare set of keys or was very skilled with a picklock. Mr Greylag," he turned to the club treasurer, "apart from you, who has the keys to this room?"

"The president and the secretary," Greylag replied. "There's also an extra set hanging in the caretaker's room."

"In other words, it's not hard to come by the keys," the detective observed. "Well, let's take a look inside. Please open the door."

Greylag obliged, and they entered a large room that looked like something between an office and a games room. In the centre was a table with a chessboard laid out on it. One corner was occupied by a huge tile stove, another by a desk, and in between them was a big cabinet with pull-down shutters. The opposite wall was decorated with framed certificates and mottoes of this sort:

Some people love money, others success,
But we in this club have a passion for chess!

Reading these words, Ambrosius smiled, but he quickly grew serious again and walked over to the desk, on which sat the cash box with its broken lock. He examined the box and muttered something under his breath before his attention was drawn to the wastepaper basket next to the desk. He bent down and pulled a torn newspaper out of it. It was *The Voice of Ashworth* from five days earlier. Ambrosius looked at it for a while before folding it neatly and putting it in his pocket. Only Cody noticed the flash of triumph in his eyes that accompanied this simple action – and realized that Ambrosius had found a clue.

A quick inspection of the windows, the table and the cabinet brought no further discoveries. However, Ambrosius grew animated again as he examined the tile stove or, more precisely, the small lumps of ash lying on the floor in front of it. A long moment passed before he stood up again.

"So? Have you found anything, Inspector?" Telesphorus Greylag couldn't help asking, intrigued by the detective's silence.

"Yes, quite a bit," Ambrosius replied tersely.

"You're very mysterious," the treasurer of the Ashworth Chess Club remarked with a crooked smile.

Ambrosius smiled back at him and replied,

"The great Hippolytus Whiskers, whom I mentioned earlier, used to teach us: 'Say little, think much and aim straight for your goal.' I follow his advice."

"But surely you can give at least a little bit away?" Greylag insisted.

"I will," Ambrosius promised. "But first I need you to answer a few questions."

"Of course, fire away!" the treasurer agreed without enthusiasm. "Shall we sit down?" He pointed to the two chairs at the table.

They settled down and Cody stretched out by Ambrosius's feet.

"Can you tell me," Ambrosius began gently, "when was the last time you were in this room?"

"Today. I've told you already. I came here earlier and discovered that someone had broken into the cash box," Greylag replied.

"Yes, I remember," Ambrosius nodded. "But what I mean is, when was the last time you were here before that?"

"Exactly a week ago," came the immediate answer.

"I come here every Wednesday to accept membership fee payments."

"Are you sure?"

Greylag hesitated for a moment, then said, "Yes, I'm sure."

"Besides you, is there anyone else who might have come into this room in the past week?"

"No. It's holiday time. The president and the secretary are both at the seaside, and even the cleaner is away. That's why nobody discovered the break-in earlier."

Ambrosius thought about something, nodded again and asked, "So when was the cleaner here last?"

"A week ago. Same as me. She said that she wanted to do a thorough cleaning before going on holiday."

"Is she a conscientious person?"

Greylag didn't understand the question.

"What I mean is, is she diligent – does she do a good and careful job of cleaning?"

"Yes, very."

"Thank you. That'll be all."

Greylag looked at Ambrosius expectantly. After a pause, he said, "You promised to share some of your findings with me..."

"I will," Ambrosius replied. "But I've just had a crazy idea: let's play a game of chess first!"

Telesphorus Greylag was speechless. He seemed to be wondering if the heat of the day hadn't affected the detective's brain.

"A game of chess? Now?" he finally managed to say.

"Yes," Ambrosius confirmed, with the expression of a mischievous rascal who had just told a very funny joke. "It's not every day that one has a chance to go up against the winner of the Golden Pawn!"

"Well, if it means so much to you..." the chess champion graciously agreed.

They drew their chairs closer to the table, reset the pieces on the chessboard and began playing. Watching from the sidelines, Cody, who at first couldn't grasp the point of Ambrosius's bizarre idea, began to understand what the detective had in mind. This wasn't an ordinary game of chess: this was a warm-up for an altogether different sort of contest, which was about to take place.

Having reached this conclusion, Cody watched the two players with increased interest. Over the course of a few minutes, Ambrosius seemed to change beyond recognition: he no longer looked like the kind-hearted detective who liked to play the flute in his spare time. His expression was determined, his gestures energetic, his moves well thought-out... His whole manner radiated confidence that he was going to win. That he had to win!

Telesphorus Greylag, on the other hand, was playing disgracefully. He was nervous and kept missing things, making moves that were unworthy of a champion. At first Ambrosius seemed not to notice, but when the winner of the Golden Pawn made a particularly inept move, the detective raised his head, looked his opponent straight in the eye and said, "You're very nervous, Mr Greylag."

Cody focused all his attention because he knew that the decisive moment had come.

Greylag replied in an unpleasant tone, "Are you surprised? You'd be nervous too if you were in my place."

Without taking his eyes off him, Ambrosius said emphatically, "You're right. If I were in your place, I'd be even more nervous."

Greylag's eyes flashed anxiously.

"What's that supposed to mean?" he asked.

"That you've lost, Mr Greylag!"

"Ah, I think you're celebrating too soon!" the treasurer cried out with relief. "The game isn't over yet."

"I'm not talking about the chess game," Ambrosius explained. "I'm talking about the game you've been playing with me for the past couple of hours."

This time, Greylag went pale.

"What on earth are you talking about?! Speak plainly, please."

"Fine, I'll speak plainly," Ambrosius agreed. "You're a thief, Mr Greylag!"

The treasurer of the Ashworth Chess Club sprung up from his seat so abruptly that he nearly knocked over the table.

"You must be mad!" He started waving his arms around. "This is a serious insult! I'll take you to court!"

Ambrosius listened to his shouting with a serene expression. When Greylag was finished, he said, "I haven't gone mad. It was you who robbed the cash box. You!" he pointed his index finger at him.

Greylag regained his composure, sat back down and only now assumed the appearance of a player who wants to win at any cost, despite having a slim chance of success.

"Do you realize," he said, "that such a serious accusation requires proof?"

"Do you really think that I would make it if I didn't have proof?" Ambrosius answered with a question.

Greylag shrugged contemptuously.

"What proof could you have? Where would you have found it?"

"I didn't need to work very hard to find it. You prepared it for me yourself."

"I'm really not in the mood for jokes right now!" Greylag snapped.

Ambrosius sighed.

"I see you're slow on the uptake. That's too bad. I'll explain everything to you as if to a child."

"You can explain it to me however you like, as long as I finally understand what you're on about."

Ambrosius settled more comfortably in his chair, took his ever-present pipe out of his pocket, filled it with tobacco, lit it and began.

"I first suspected you back at my flat, when you were so worried about your good reputation and so unconcerned about the stolen money. That seemed strange to me. For a person with a clear conscience, it would have been the opposite way around, don't you agree?"

"Perhaps," Greylag grunted. "But my good reputation is more important to me than money. And in any case, that isn't proof!"

"Of course not," the detective agreed. "I'm not calling it proof either; I'm just sharing my observations with you. By the way, there's something else you were careless about, which is another strike against you."

"This is getting better and better!" Greylag snarled with disdain. "I'm curious now!"

"When I asked you if anyone else might have come into this room in the past week, you said – and I quote – 'No. It's holiday time. The president and the secretary are both at the seaside, and even the cleaner is away. That's why nobody discovered the break-in earlier.' This answer could have been given only by someone who knew that the break-in had taken place a few days ago – five, to be precise. And only the thief knew that!"

"Well, well, look at that – you even know the date of the theft!" Greylag sneered, but he seemed to be breathing faster.

"As you'll see in a minute, I know more than the date," the detective replied and continued. "Back in my flat in Lilac Street, I quoted to you my friend's words about how ghosts never leave traces but people always do. As usual, he was right. You also left traces. Two different ones."

This time Greylag didn't sneer. He looked like somebody expecting a blow.

"The first was this newspaper." Ambrosius took the piece of *The Voice of Ashworth* out of his pocket and waved it in front of Greylag. "You said that the last time you were here was a week ago. So how did your paper from five days ago end up in this room?"

"How do you know that it was mine?" Greylag said indignantly. "Nearly everyone in this town reads *The Voice of Ashworth!*"

"Indeed," Ambrosius nodded. "But not every copy has your name handwritten on it by the postman. And here it is. There is not a shadow of doubt that the newspaper was yours and that you left it here five days ago, when you came to rob the cash box. So now you know how I got the date of the theft."

"I could have left it here today," Greylag said in a less confident tone. "As you know, I was here earlier..."

Ambrosius narrowed his eyes and looked at him ironically.

"You've been carrying a newspaper for five days, only to throw it into the bin here, today?"

Greylag didn't reply.

"In any case, the newspaper came in very handy," the detective continued. "When you opened the cash box and took out the money, you started looking around for something to wrap it in. There was nothing handy lying about, so you remembered about the newspaper. You took it out of your pocket, tore off half the front page and used it to wrap the banknotes. Then you threw out the rest. Unfortunately for you!"

Greylag regained his ability to talk.

"You have the strangest ideas!" he cried out. "Why would have I wrapped the money in a newspaper? I could've easily just put it in a briefcase or in my pocket, without wrapping it."

"No doubt that's what you would have done," Ambrosius said, "if you had been bold enough to take the money home. But you were afraid. For the time being, you preferred to hide it here, in this room. Or, to be more precise, inside this stove!"

Ambrosius pointed to the huge tile stove in the corner, while Greylag gripped the edge of the table and looked close to fainting.

"How did you discover that?" he finally managed to say, confirming the detective's guess.

"It was very easy," Ambrosius said. "On the floor next to the stove, I noticed small lumps of ash – the second trace you left. I started wondering where this ash could have come from, since nobody lights a stove at this time of year, and with a diligent cleaner, who comes here once a week, there's no chance that the ash has lain there since the winter. The conclusion was obvious: somebody must have looked inside the stove. Why? To burn or to hide something. Do you see now?"

Telesphorus Greylag was crushed. He realized that he had lost, and lost badly! There was nothing he could say in his defence. He shrunk into himself, put his head in his hands and remained like that for a while, thinking bitter thoughts.

Ambrosius looked at Cody. They understood each other without words. *It's always the same,* their eyes said. *First there's the great self-confidence, and then regret, which always comes too late.*

At long last, Greylag raised his head.

"What are you planning to do now?" he asked.

"There's only one thing I can do: inform the police," Ambrosius replied in his usual gentle voice.

Greylag nodded, resigned.

"I'll never be the president now..." he said, more to himself than to Mr Nosegoode, and put his face in his hands again.

THE SAD END OF THE ELUSIVE HAND

The day before the opening of a grand exhibition titled Celebrating One Hundred Years of Ashworth, Detective Ambrosius Nosegoode received a letter. At the sight of the envelope, his heart beat faster because he recognized the familiar handwriting of his great teacher and friend Hippolytus Whiskers.

"Hippo has written!" he called out to Cody, who was gnawing on a rabbit thigh with gusto.

Cody abandoned his treat, which was something he almost never did, and within seconds was standing next to Ambrosius.

"Read it!" he panted, licking the grease off his chin.

Ambrosius tore open the envelope, unfolded the piece of paper, cleared his throat and began reading aloud.

My Dear Friend!

I'm sorry to disturb the festive atmosphere of Ashworth's centenary celebrations with my troublesome message, but – as you well know – for me duty always comes first. I'm writing to tell you that I found out from certain sources, which I don't want to name here, that a certain disagreeable character – a well-known pickpocket called the Elusive Hand – is planning to come to the opening of your big exhibition. As his nickname suggests, he is a cunning criminal who is very difficult to catch. Suffice it to say that I have never managed it myself. I hope that you, my friend, might have better luck. Indeed, I wish it with all my heart.

The task of catching the Elusive Hand is all the more difficult because of the ease with which he assumes different disguises. One day he's a retired professor, the next day a beggar, and once he even appeared in the role of a rather large female market trader. The only things he cannot seem to change are his height and his bulk, which is why I must tell you that he's about six feet tall and weighs well over fifteen stone. Watch out for people of that build.

I'm sorry that I've dedicated most of my letter to a person who is not worthy of it, but this is an important matter. I solemnly promise you that next time I'll write more about myself.

In closing, I send you my warmest greetings, and as for your invaluable assistant Cody, I wish him a life strewn with bones.

Your devoted friend,
            Hippolytus

"Hippo is great!" Cody declared when Ambrosius had finished. "He's truly great!"

"Because he's written to let us know about the Elusive Hand's upcoming guest appearances?" Ambrosius asked innocently.

Cody didn't detect the gentle sarcasm in his tone and answered sincerely.

"Are you kidding? It's because he sent me such beautiful wishes! A life strewn with bones..." his voice grew dreamy. "Could there be anything more wonderful?"

"That depends for whom," Ambrosius muttered.

Cody was irritated.

"Ah, talking to people about bones is like talking to pigs about flying. We'd better discuss the Elusive Hand instead."

It was Ambrosius's turn become dreamy.

"If only we could manage to catch him..." He sighed.

"I have a feeling we will!" Cody's eyes lit up. "My nose tells me so. We just have to approach this matter with our heads screwed on. Let's think for a bit."

Since Mr Nosegoode had nothing against thinking, both of them devoted themselves to this useful activity for some time. Then they had a long discussion about what to do next, which Ambrosius summarized in his notebook as follows:

1. *Go to the opening of the exhibition.*

2. *Closely observe all strangers who are six feet tall and weigh about fifteen stone.*

3. *Determine which of them is the Elusive Hand.*

4. *Follow the Elusive Hand's every move.*

5. *Catch the Elusive Hand red-handed.*

6. *Hand him over to the police.*

The plan was remarkably simple. It was true that some of the points were easier to note down than to put into practice, but – as Cody often said – difficult problems were like bones: they were there to be cracked.

Ambrosius shared this view, so they went to bed in an excellent mood. Yet, as it happened, the elusive pickpocket tormented them both during the night. In Cody's dreams he assumed the shape of the caretaker of their building, while to Ambrosius he appeared dressed as a pharaoh. The morning, however, restored their good spirits.

Exchanging friendly banter, as usual, they quickly ate breakfast and left their flat at nine o'clock.

Outside, they were greeted by a festive hubbub. Streamers trailed down from windows and balconies, colourful banners hung suspended above the streets and, underneath it all, large groups of people hurried towards the market square, where the exhibition hall was located. Ambrosius and Cody joined this celebratory throng and let it carry them in the same direction.

It was half past nine when they reached the square: thirty minutes before the opening ceremony was due to start. They had been planning to wander around for a while, observing people, but the crowd was growing thicker and thicker, so they found a spot near the podium and decided to await the arrival of the mayor, who was supposed to open the exhibition.

The mayor appeared at five to ten. He arrived in a low, black carriage and mounted the podium with the look of great solemnity on his face and a shiny top hat on his head. General applause and a loud fanfare from the fire brigade's orchestra welcomed him to the stage. He listened graciously and then raised his hand to signal that he wanted to speak. A hush descended over the spectators, and out flowed a stream of lofty words about the hundred-year-old town – about its history, its beauty and its achievements, about the hard work of its inhabitants and the wisdom of its government... The mayor's speech was so uplifting that it seemed as if at any moment he might rise into the air and, despite his considerable weight, float up towards the clouds. Fortunately, things didn't go that far, and he spoke on, inspiring feelings of great pride in the hearts of even the most modest of Ashworth's residents.

After the speech, which was followed by another round of applause and another fanfare from the orchestra, the mayor descended the steps, went up to the ribbon in front of the entrance to the hall and cut it with a huge pair of scissors, which had been handed to him by a girl dressed in a local folk costume.

With the exhibition hall now open, Ambrosius and Cody could proceed with their plan. First, however, as proud residents of Ashworth, they decided to take a look at the displays.

"I don't think the thief will start picking pockets while the mayor is here," Ambrosius said hopefully.

Trusting that he was right, they entered the hall. The exhibition was divided into three parts: "The History of Our Town", "Famous Residents" and "Handmade in Ashworth". They visited each in turn. The first part featured old photographs, objects and documents illustrating the town's history. The most interesting item on display was the hundred-year-old mallet that had been used to hammer in the stakes to mark out the future town square. A century later, it made for a touching sight.

The main attraction in the second part was the gallery of portraits of Ashworth's greatest inhabitants. One painting in particular stood out: the portrait of Polycarp Squint, the inventor of rose-coloured spectacles. The painter had skilfully captured the untroubled cheerfulness emanating from the inventor's face. Regrettably, following established custom, portraits of living people had not been allowed in the exhibition. If it hadn't been for that, the gallery would no doubt have included Detective Ambrosius Nosegoode. Or at least that was what Cody maintained, despite his master's feeble protests.

The third part of the exhibition showcased the work of local artisans. Among the items on display were elegant shoes and ingenious money pouches, the famous crescent-shaped Ashworth rolls and confectioners' masterpieces, beautiful gold jewellery and wonders made from wrought iron – dozens upon dozens of objects, all showing the great skill and artistry of Ashworth's craftspeople.

Ambrosius was looking at ornate locks laid out in one of the display cases when he heard a piercing shriek coming from just a few steps away.

"My watch!" somebody cried. "My watch has been stolen!"

So the Elusive Hand is here and he's begun his work! Ambrosius thought and within seconds he was standing beside the victim. He quickly looked all around and saw three people who, judging by their appearance, could be the elusive thief. The first was a tall, stout woman with a distinct hint of a moustache under her nose, an umbrella in her hand and a huge hat covered all over with what appeared to be real flowers. The second was a man in a baggy grey raincoat gazing indifferently at a nearby display case with his hands folded behind his back. The third was an individual who looked like... a retired professor. He was busily looking all around.

"One of these three must be the Elusive Hand," Ambrosius whispered to Cody. "Let's start by investigating the woman with the botanical garden on her head. She'll be the easiest to check: we just need to hear her voice."

The woman, as if sensing that she was the focus of attention, elbowed her way out of the crowd of onlookers and headed for the exit. Without a moment's hesitation, Ambrosius and his dog followed.

"She's marching like a soldier on parade," Cody muttered.

They laughed and hastened their steps.

When they caught up with her, Ambrosius tipped his hat and addressed her in the most charming voice he could muster.

"Pardon me, madam, but are you by any chance the daffodil lady?"

The words were barely out of his mouth when he regretted them.

"What did you say?! Daft old lady?" she yelled loud enough for the whole square to hear. She gave him a withering look and raised her umbrella. "Listen, you'd better scram, or I'll teach you a lesson you'll never forget!"

It was a woman – there was no doubt of that.

Ambrosius had no intention of taking lessons from the combative lady – he instantly made a dash for it. When he reached a safe distance, he stopped, wiped his sweaty forehead and heaved a dramatic sigh.

"Dear, oh dear! What a dangerous job this tracking down of criminals is!"

Both he and Cody burst out laughing again and decided to turn their attention to the next suspect: the retired professor. They went back into the exhibition hall, where they had no trouble picking out the large figure in the crowd. He was standing in front of a case with gold jewellery, pretending to be examining its contents, but any attentive observer could easily see that his eyes kept darting nervously left and right.

"A suspicious-looking sort," Cody said with conviction.

Ambrosius didn't contradict him, and they began following the 'professor'. They paused to look at the same display cases, sat down for a little rest on adjacent benches, drank orangeade from the same stalls...

After two hours of wandering around town during which nothing unusual happened, the 'professor' clearly got hungry and he went into the Hambone Inn. As they followed him inside, Cody was torn. *Somebody who's planning to eat dinner in the company of dogs*, he reasoned, *cannot be a bad person.* But then he remembered how he first met Beanpole and Doughnut in the very same pub, and his suspicions instantly returned.

Cody didn't have time to ponder this further, however, because the 'professor' noticed them. He nearly choked at the sight of them, astonished, but his expression soon changed to that of anger. He stared at Mr Nosegoode for a few seconds and then seemed to come to a decision. He got up abruptly from his table and strode over to them looking like a storm cloud.

"Thundering pork chops!" he boomed. "Who are you, and why are you trailing after me, like a fox chasing a goose?"

His roaring didn't make much of an impression on Mr Nosegoode. He looked the 'professor' straight in the eye and wondered who he was dealing with: an exceptionally bold criminal or a completely innocent man.

When the rumbling died down, the detective said, "Before I answer your questions, I have two requests. First, could you please speak more quietly? I suffered from ear infections as a child, and ever since then I can't stand shouting. And second, please sit down because I don't like people towering over me."

Ambrosius's calm, dignified manner served to cool the man's temper. He gasped, letting go of the last of his anger, stepped back and sank into a chair.

"Fine. I'll do as you ask. Now can you finally tell me what you want from me? Are you playing cops and robbers with me or what?"

Ambrosius looked at him with a start. Was it a

coincidence, this mention of cops and robbers, or a calculated move?

He assumed a mysterious expression and replied, "Perhaps..."

The man's face twisted into what was probably meant to be a smile.

"Let's play then, robber!" he said.

"Why would I be the robber?" Ambrosius asked. "Wouldn't that role suit you better?"

"No!" said the 'professor' decisively. "I can't be anything other than a policeman."

"And why is that?"

"Because I *am* a policeman," came the astonishing reply. "I've been a policeman for thirty years!"

Ambrosius was dumbfounded.

"You're... you're a policeman?" he managed to say at last.

The man chuckled.

"What did you think: that you were talking to the Emperor of China?"

Ambrosius still wasn't quite convinced.

"Could I see your ID?" he asked.

"Of course."

The 'professor' fished the document out of his pocket and presented it to Mr Nosegoode.

"Inspector Balthazar Bee," Ambrosius read out in a low voice. Then he burst into uncontrollable laughter.

Balthazar Bee looked at him with distaste.

"You have a rather strange sense of humour," he remarked.

Ambrosius used the back of his hand to wipe the tears from his eyes.

"We can talk about my sense of humour in a minute," he said. "But first I'd like you to take a look at this!" He handed the inspector his own ID.

The roles were now reversed. The policeman looked at the document, blinked in surprise, looked up at Mr Nosegoode and exclaimed, "So you are Ambrosius Nosegoode?! The famous detective?"

Ambrosius nodded, highly amused.

It was only now, when no doubts remained as to who was who, that Balthazar Bee roared with laughter, so loudly that all the eyes in the room turned towards them. Ambrosius joined him, and for a few minutes they sat at the table howling without restraint. Cody, too, shared in their merriment.

The first to compose himself was Balthazar Bee.

"Well, now that we each know who the other is," he began, "perhaps you can tell me why you've been shadowing me for the past two hours?"

Ambrosius was embarrassed.

"I thought that you might be a famous pickpocket whom I wanted to catch red-handed," he confessed. "I was given a physical description of him, and you fit that description..."

"Are you talking about the Elusive Hand?" the policeman's interest was aroused.

"Yes. Do you know him?" It was Ambrosius's turn to be curious.

"Do I know him? Of course! That's the whole reason I've come to this town. My goal is the same as yours: to catch him in the act of stealing."

"Was he the man in the baggy grey raincoat standing close to you when the watch was stolen?"

"Yes. But he wasn't the one who stole that watch. I observed him closely from the moment he came in. I didn't take my eyes off his hands even for a second, and I can guarantee that those hands couldn't have stolen a thing. The Elusive Hand kept them firmly behind his back the entire time, as if he wanted to show the whole world that he had no intention whatsoever of stealing."

"Strange," Ambrosius said thoughtfully. "This suggests that the Elusive Hand doesn't act alone."

"Yes, it would seem so," the inspector agreed. "But we can't check on that while sitting in this cosy pub. I propose that we go back to the exhibition and take another look around."

"Should we go back together?" Ambrosius asked.

"No, separately. I'll wander around the exhibits, and you can focus on the Elusive Hand. Sooner or later, he's bound to reach into somebody's pocket."

"Wouldn't you rather be the one keeping an eye on him?" replied Ambrosius. "After all, that's why you've come..."

"No," Balthazar Bee cut him off. "It's better that you do it. He might recognize me, since we live in the same town."

"Very well," Ambrosius said, "I'll gladly go after him myself."

After agreeing on a time and place to meet, they parted like good friends, and Ambrosius and Cody headed back to the market.

It was still bustling with people. Groups of visitors thronged to the exhibition hall while others, leaving, spilled out into the square. Friendly greetings mingled with the shouts of market traders, who had laid out their wares and were touting everything from large gingerbread hearts to fly traps.

The Elusive Hand was in the crowd as well. Ambrosius noticed him as he approached a bearded artist who was drawing portraits. The thief pushed his way into the cluster of onlookers surrounding the artist and stood watching with his hands folded behind his back.

Ambrosius bent down towards Cody.

"Pay attention to his hands," he whispered. "Don't let them out of your sight for even a second!"

Cody nodded.

Meanwhile, the Elusive Hand had moved suspiciously close to a young man who was posing for a portrait. He watched for a time as the artist sketched the outline of the young man's face, then he yawned widely and slowly walked off. Ambrosius was going to follow him, but first he wanted to see for himself what a portrait drawn so quickly might look like. He slipped into the spot that the thief had left a moment earlier and spent a few minutes admiring the artist's skill. It wasn't long before the portrait was finished, and its owner reached into his pocket to pay for it. His hand froze inside and he went pale. The pocket was empty.

After rummaging around in vain for a moment, the young man cried out, "I've been robbed! My money is gone!"

Ambrosius didn't stay to listen to what came next. He signalled to Cody, and they set off in pursuit of the Elusive Hand.

"Did you watch his hands?" he asked the dog.

"Yes, just like you said. They never moved from behind his back. He couldn't have stolen the money."

"So who did?" Ambrosius frowned. "Only he could have reached into that young man's pocket without being seen. He was standing right next to him."

"What if someone else had robbed the young man earlier?" Cody thought out loud. "It didn't have to happen then and there."

"That's what I thought too," the detective replied. "But it can't be a coincidence that whenever something goes missing the Elusive Hand is right next to the victim. There must be more to this, but what?"

For now they had no answer. But they also had no trouble finding the Elusive Hand, who this time appeared to be interested in an acrobatic display being put on by the local athletics club.

Ambrosius sat down on a bench a few yards away from the athletes and continued racking his brains over the mysterious thefts. *What's the secret?* he wondered. *I saw with my own eyes that he didn't steal that money, and yet I'm sure that he did.*

An urgent tug on his sleeve interrupted his thoughts. Cody seemed greatly agitated by something and was gesturing to him incomprehensibly.

"What's going on?" Ambrosius asked, not seeing anything suspicious.

"His hands!" Cody whispered. "Look at his hands!"

"I don't see anything unusual," Ambrosius strained his eyes. "They're in the same place as before."

"Come on!" the dog grew impatient. "The wasp! Can't you see the wasp?"

Indeed! A wasp was slowly crawling up the thief's left hand and he didn't make the slightest move.

"It's impossible for him not to feel that!" Cody said. "Why doesn't he move his hand and shake it off?"

Ambrosius nodded and concentrated, thinking as hard as he could. He felt that he was on the verge of solving the mystery – that in a moment the dark wall he had been trying to break through would finally crack apart.

"I've got it!" he suddenly let out of a muffled cry. "I've found the solution! It's so simple! But if you hadn't seen that wasp, my friend, I would have never thought of it. You really deserve a huge bone!"

"You have to explain!" Cody licked his lips.

"Not yet," Ambrosius brushed him off. "First we must quickly find Balthazar Bee and... a decent apple!"

"What?!" Cody looked at him goggle-eyed.

"An apple. An ordinary apple," Ambrosius repeated and sprang up from the bench.

Events unfolded with lightning speed. Ambrosius found Inspector Bee inside the hall, quickly bought an apple from a startled vendor and – with his purchase in his pocket and with Cody and Balthazar Bee by his side – hurried off to meet the Elusive Hand.

"What's the meaning of all this?" the policeman wanted to know. "What are you planning to do?"

Ambrosius's face lit up with a proud smile.

"Unmask the Elusive Hand!" he replied and turned a deaf ear to all further questions.

The pickpocket must have got bored of athletics. He was now sitting and taking in the sun on the very same bench where Mr Nosegoode had made his remarkable discovery. His hands were still behind his back, exactly as before, and his face radiated deep satisfaction. He noticed the two men and the dog coming towards him, but he didn't pay them much attention.

Meanwhile, Cody and the inspectors were growing more and more excited. Ambrosius tightened his grip on the apple in his pocket. Balthazar Bee and Cody began to sweat. They knew that something extraordinary was about to take place, but they had no idea what it would be.

They were now only a step away from the bench where the Elusive Hand was sitting.

And then it happened! Ambrosius quickly pulled the apple out of his pocket and, shouting "Catch!", tossed it at the thief. That very second, an astonishing thing occurred: a pair of hands popped out of the baggy raincoat and caught the apple. The other pair of hands remained motionless behind the thief's back...

"The game is up, Elusive Hand!" Detective Nosegoode cried out triumphantly.

The thief didn't even try to defend himself. He realized that the finely made fake hands, which he wore behind his back to avoid being discovered, were undeniable proof of his criminal activities...

So that was the end of the Elusive Hand's career –
and yet another great success for Detective Ambrosius
Nosegoode and his dog. The solving of this difficult
case – like the ones before – amazed the whole
town of Ashworth and brought the two friends
well-deserved fame.

PUSHKIN CHILDREN'S BOOKS

We created Pushkin Children's Books to share tales from different languages and cultures with younger readers, and to open the door to the wide, colourful worlds these stories offer.

From picture books and adventure stories to fairy tales and classics, and from fifty-year-old bestsellers to current huge successes abroad, the books on the Pushkin Children's list reflect the very best stories from around the world, for our most discerning readers of all: children.